The Hopes and Dreams Series
Salvadoran-Americans

Neighbors

A story based on history

T0164531

Tana Reiff

Illustrations by Tyler Stiene

PR●● LiNGUA
LEARNING

Pro Lingua Learning

P.O. Box 4467
Rockville, Maryland 20849
Office: 1-301-424-8900
Book orders: 1-800-888-4741
Web: ProLinguaLearning.com
Email: Info@ProLinguaLearning.com

Copyright © 1993, 2019 by Tana Reiff

Text ISBN 978-0-86647-487-0

The cover and illustrations are by Tyler Stiene. The book was set and designed by Tana Reiff, consulting with A.A. Burrows, using the Adobe *Century Schoolbook* typeface for the text. This is a digital adaptation of one of the most popular faces of the twentieth century. Century's distinctive roman and italic fonts and its clear, dark strokes and serifs were designed, as the name suggests, to make schoolbooks easy to read. The display font used on the cover and titles is a 21st-century digital invention titled Telugu. It is designed to work on all digital platforms and with Indic scripts. Telugu is named for the Telugu people in southern India and their widely spoken language. This is a simple, strong, and interesting sans serif display font.

Audio MP3 files for this book are available for purchase and download at ProLinguaLearning.com/audio.

The Hopes and Dreams Series
by Tana Reiff

The Magic Paper (Mexican-Americans)
For Gold and Blood (Chinese-Americans)
Nobody Knows (African-Americans)
Little Italy (Italian-Americans)
Hungry No More (Irish-Americans)
Sent Away (Japanese-Americans)
Two Hearts (Greek-Americans)
A Different Home (Cuban-Americans)
The Family from Vietnam (Vietnamese-Americans)
Old Ways, New Ways (Jewish-Americans)
Amala's Hope (A Family from Syria)
Neighbors (A Family from El Salvador)

Contents

1   Ramón and Pilar

El Salvador, Central America, 1980

Óscar Romero,
Archbishop of San Salvador,
had more than Mass
to say today.

"I speak
to the army and police,"
Archbishop Romero began.
"We are all the same people.
You are killing
your own brother peasants.
Remember the voice of God:
'Thou shalt not kill.'
God's law must win.
In the name of God,
I beg you.
Stop the war!"*

*Adapted from the actual words of
Óscar Arnulfo Romero, Archbishop of
San Salvador, in his radio sermon on
March 23, 1980, the day before his death.*

All of a sudden,
a man burst in.
He fired a gun
straight at Archbishop Romero.
The archbishop fell to the floor,
shot in the heart.
His blood
turned his white clothes red.
He died on the spot.

News of Romero's death
spread throughout El Salvador.
Ramón and Pilar Samoya
in their village
near the city of San Miguel
heard about it on the radio.

The Samoyas
were young *campesinos*,
peasant farm workers.
Their house was made
of sticks and mud.
Ramón farmed
a little piece of land.
He grew corn
like the other farmers
in the village.

Pilar took care
of their two small children.
She carried water
from the river.
She ground corn
with a rock.
She cooked
on a round iron pan
over a wood fire.
Chickens and pigs
ran around the yard.
The young Samoya family
worked very hard.
Their life was simple but happy.
Until now.

Ramón and Pilar
knew about the civil war
in El Salvador.
They were surprised to hear
the Archbishop's strong words
against the new government.

"Archbishop Romero
is right,"
Ramón said.
"The killing must end.
It is time for peace."

"Are we safe
here in our village?"
Pilar asked her husband.

"No one is safe,"
said Ramón.

"I have heard
of very bad things
happening to people,"
said Pilar.
"Some people
have disappeared!"

"People say 'disappeared',"
said Ramón.
"But it means dead.
The government
is the army,"
Ramón went on.
"Their 'death squads'
go out and kill people.
A death squad
killed the Archbishop.
Then there are the *guerillas*.
They are against the government.
But they hurt and kill too."

"Is it safe for us
to talk about this?"
asked Pilar.

"I don't know,"
said Ramón.
"We should watch our words.
There are birds in the field.**
We can only hope
some good will come
of the Archbishop's death.
Maybe now the world
will hear what's going on
in El Salvador."

**The English version of this expression is
(Be quiet.) "The walls have ears."

2 Felipe

Over the next few months,
Ramón and Pilar
heard more stories.
Army death squads
were coming into villages
and killing people.
These stories were never
heard on the radio.
But word got around,
from person to person,
from village to village.

In some places,
guerilla forces
kept the government away.
Then the police
or a death squad
would show up
to fight the *guerillas*.
Many people were killed.
Some were killed
for speaking out
against the government.

Whole villages were burned
to the ground
for no clear reason.
This was war.

One night,
as the Samoya family slept,
Pilar heard screams.
All of a sudden,
she was wide-awake.
The screams were coming
from a neighbor's home.
Then she heard gunshots.
When the shooting stopped,
so did the screams.

"Ramón! Ramón!"
Pilar cried.
She shook her husband's arm.

"What's going on?"
Ramón asked.

"Outside!
Someone has been shot!"
cried Pilar.

Ramón looked outside.
He saw a big black dog
running toward their neighbor's home.
It was the black *cadejo**,
the force of evil.
The devil.
El cadejo was not real,
and yet it was.

Then Ramón and Pilar
heard a man's voice.
"You, *campesino*!
Come with us!"

"No, no,"
their neighbor Felipe begged.

*The legend of El Cadejo is very popular
in El Salvador and other parts of
Central America and South America.
Native ancestors believed the dog helped
people into the afterlife when they died.
When the Spaniards and Christianity
came to these places, the legend changed
to show the difference between good
(a white dog) and evil (a black dog).*

"They are taking him away!"
said Ramón.
"Why? Why?
And look!
His house is on fire!"

In no time at all
the little house
was a ball of fire.

Pilar began to cry.
"We are poor *campesinos*.
Why do they do this
to people like us?"

"Maybe Felipe
worked for the wrong people,"
said Ramón.
"Or maybe he did nothing.
I only wish
we could have helped
our neighbors."

3 The Land

Their neighbor's home
was gone.
Felipe's wife was dead.
And Felipe had "disappeared."

Ramón looked
at the ashes on the ground.
"So this is how
a death squad works,"
he said sadly.

Village life carried on.
But a short time later,
word came
that the land would be taken.
The *campesinos*
held a meeting.

"We have always farmed,"
said one man.
"If we must leave,
what will we do?"

"We have three choices,"
said one man.
"We can do farm work
somewhere else.
We can go to the city
and look for work.
Or we can join the army."

"Three bad choices,"
said Ramón.
"Farming somewhere else
may be no safer than here.
There are not enough jobs
in the city.
And I will not join the army
and kill Salvadorans!"

"If we stay here,
they will come and kill us!"
said another man.

"Then so be it!"
shouted Ramón.

As soon as he spoke,
he felt afraid.
What if the wrong people
found out he had said that?
He sat on his mat
and said nothing else.

Over the next weeks,
people began to leave the village.
The Samoyas stayed.

But then Ramón did something
he had never dreamed of.
He and some other *campesinos*
went to San Salvador,
the capital city.
They marched
against the government.
No one shot at them.
However, Ramón saw someone
taking pictures.
That made him afraid.

A few days after that,
a group of *guerillas*
came to the village.

Their faces were covered.
They carried machine guns.
"You must join us,"
they told Ramón.
"We will help you
stay on this land."

"I don't want to join,"
said Ramón.
"I don't want to be
on one side or the other.
I just want
to farm this land."

One of the *guerillas*
grabbed Ramón's arms.
"Think it over, my friend,"
said the *guerilla*.
"Think it over well!"

Ramón went home
and told Pilar
about the *guerillas*.
"All I want is to farm
this little piece of land.
Is that too much to ask?"

"Stop!" called the old man.
"He is a hard-working
campesino.
Nothing else.
Don't kill him."

"Who are you?"
a soldier asked the old man.

"I have known Ramón
all his life.
He is my neighbor,"
said the old man.
"He has nothing to do
with the guerillas."

The soldier took his foot
off Ramón's head.
"Today you may go free,"
said the soldier.
"But if you know
what is good for you,
you will get out of here.
If you stay,
we will kill you.
We will give your bones
back to the earth!"

Then he kicked Ramón,
and the soldiers drove off.

   Ramón finished walking
back to the village.
His head
was covered with blood.

   He stayed up all night,
thinking about his next steps.
Ramón would never forgot
what his neighbor said:
"He is my neighbor."
But he knew
what he had to do.

   "I must leave here,"
he told Pilar sadly.
"You and the children
will stay.
The trip will be too hard.
I will come back
as soon as things cool off."

5 Leaving the Country

Ramón put some things
into a little bag.
He walked to San Miguel.
There, he got a visa
to visit Mexico.
Then he took a bus
headed north
through Guatemala
and then into Mexico.
From Mexico,
he hoped to cross the border
into the United States.

Ramón sat on the bus
and looked out the window.
He saw the beautiful green land
and high mountains
of El Salvador.
He saw burned homes and trees.
He saw soldiers
standing along the road.

"Why must they fight
over this beautiful country?"
he said to himself.

The miles passed,
one by one by one.
Ramón changed buses
along the way.
With each different bus,
he felt farther and farther away
from Pilar and the children.
He worried about them
every minute.

Days later,
in the north of Mexico,
Ramón got off the bus.
He was close to the U.S. now.

He walked the back roads.
He stopped at houses
to ask for food.
But he was still hungry.
His stomach was never full.
And he was very, very tired.

It was night
when he reached the Rio Grande.
The United States
was on the other side
of the river.
The young *campesino*
felt alone and afraid.
He knew he would not be safe
without papers in the U.S.
But he would be safer
than a man marked for death
in his own country.

When he thought
that no one was looking,
he made the sign of the cross.
He took off his shoes
and put them in his bag.
He held the bag
between his teeth.
He walked down the bank
into the river.
The river was not wide here.
It was not deep.
However, it was
over his head.
Ramón was able to swim across
in a few minutes.

He climbed the bank
on the other side.
When he looked up
he saw two men
and the black *cadejo*
coming toward him.
They tied his hands
behind his back
and pushed him
into a truck.
The U.S. Border Patrol
had stopped Ramón.

The border patrol
put Ramón in jail.
"Please don't send me
back to El Salvador,"
Ramón begged.
"I will be killed!"

"That's what they all say!"
said the men.
"Here, sign this."

6 Back Again

Ramón had signed
a paper in English.
It said, "I agree to return
to El Salvador."

Back in San Salvador,
Ramón walked miles and miles
to his home village.

The village was gone.
The ground was covered
with ashes.
The black *cadejo*
danced beside him.
All he found
was Pilar's iron cooking pan.
What could have happened
to his family?
He didn't want to think.
He didn't know what to do.

Ramón decided
to pay a coyote to take him
back to the U.S.
So he went
to Mexico City.
He found work.
He saved up enough money
to pay a coyote.

He got on
the coyote's van.
No seats.
No windows.
Not big enough
for all the people
packed inside it.

With each passing hour
the van grew hotter.
It smelled very bad.
It was hard to breathe.
"Please, God,"
Ramón begged.
"Don't let me die now."

A day passed
and then a night.
The next morning
the van crossed the border
into the United States.
Tired, hot, and hungry,
everyone cried for joy.

The van went
another ten miles
before coming to a stop.
The back door opened.
Then the coyote shouted,
"Everyone out!"

One by one,
people jumped out.
The van pulled away.

Ramón looked around.
The coyote had left them
in the Arizona desert.
They were on their own now.

7 Two Nuns

"What now?"
asked one woman,
who found it hard to talk.
Like the others,
she needed something to drink.

It was early morning.
The air was cool.
It felt good.
But this was the desert.
The sun rose higher.
The air got hotter.
Their skin burned.
There was no water,
only a cactus plant
here and there.

"Does anyone know
how to get juice
out of a cactus?"
someone asked.

Ramón walked over
to a tall cactus.
He took his knife
and cut off the spines.
Then he pressed the cactus.
A little bit of juice
came out.
He passed around a cup.
Over and over,
he pressed the cactus for juice
and shared with his neighbors.

The cactus juice
saved some lives that day.
But the van ride
and desert heat
were too much for some.
The women
began to pray.

By noon
the next day,
everyone was sitting
on the ground.
Everyone felt half dead.
By the end of the day
two of the older women
had died.

Ramón was the first
to hear the sound.
The first to see
the white *cadejo*.
At first he thought
it was all in his mind.
But a real white van
pulled up to the group.
Two young nuns got out
and handed out water.

"Come with us,"
said one of the nuns.
"We will take you
to a safe place."

As the van drove on,
the nuns gave out more
food and water.

They came to a house
in a small town.
The nuns
helped the people walk.
Inside were other people
from Central America—
Guatemala and Honduras.

"This is a safe house
for Central American refugees,"
said Sister Dora in Spanish.
"We will help you
back to health.
Then we will help you go
to other safe houses."

"We have no papers,"
said Ramón.

The nun smiled.
"We understand that,"
she said softly.
"That's why you need help."

8 Barney and Sarah

Ramón was in bad shape.
He needed food and water.
He needed a bath.
A doctor
gave him something
for his skin and eyes.
The nuns gave him
new clothes.

"Gracias, gracias,"
Ramon said to the nuns.
"Why do you do this?"
Ramón asked in Spanish.

"The Bible says
to love your neighbor
as yourself,"
said Sister Dora.

"In El Salvador,
I didn't know who
my neighbor was.

The *guerillas*
wanted me to join them.
The army told me
to leave the country
or I would be killed.
So here I am,
my second try.
I am lucky to be alive."

    Ramón asked
if the nuns could get him papers.

    "We would if we could,"
said Sister Dora.
"But don't apply for asylum."

    "What is asylum?"
Ramón wondered.

    "Asylum would let you
stay in the U.S.
because you are not safe
in your home country,"
said Sister Dora.
"But Salvadorans
are not being given asylum.

They will say
you came here
only to make money."

   "I came here
to stay *alive!*"
said Ramón.
"I think
that my wife and children
are already dead."

   "I am so sorry for you,"
said Sister Dora.

   A few weeks later
Sister Dora told Ramón
a family in Texas
would give him sanctuary,
a safe place to live.
"They are breaking the law,"
she explained.
"But they feel that God's law
is greater than man's.
Just like Archbishop Romero said."

Barney and Sarah Fuller
met Ramón at the bus station.
They didn't speak much Spanish.
But they and Ramón got by
with just a few words.

It was strange for Ramón
to live in this American home.
He was, after all,
a peasant from El Salvador.
He had never had
running water inside.
Or a kitchen.
Or a soft bed with sheets.
He had never eaten
the kind of food
Sarah put on the table.

When Ramón thought about
what had happened to him,
he would shake all over.
He had trouble sleeping.
He had bad dreams.
His body had gotten well.
But his mind
was still in pain.

The Fullers
found work for Ramón.
He did cleaning
at a big restaurant.
He washed dishes.
He also helped the Fullers
around the house.
He went to church with them
every Sunday.
Still, he didn't fit in.
But living "underground"
was better than not living at all.

After some time,
Ramón did get asylum.
He got a green card.
Now he could work
without fear.
He could pay U.S. taxes.
But if he ever left the U.S.
he could never come back.

Night after night,
he pushed the mop
at the restaurant.

The sound of the mop
back and forth
across the floor
seemed to be saying,
"Pilar, Pilar, Pilar."
It made him feel sad.
But the hope
of seeing Pilar
and the children again
kept him going.

9 Pilar's Story

Then one day
everything changed.

"We got a phone call today,"
Sarah began.
"From a church in Houston.
They are helping
a Salvadoran woman
and her two children.
Her name is Pilar.
But her last name is Mendez."

"That is my wife!"
cried Ramón.
"Mendez is her family name.
My Pilar is alive!"

Sarah and Barney
drove Ramón to Houston.
Their hearts burst with joy
to see the Samoya family
together again.

They hugged each other.
They didn't want to let go.
Crying. Smiling. Laughing.
Crying some more.

"What happened to you?"
Ramón asked.
"I went back to the village.
It was burned to the ground.
I thought you had disappeared."

"I did not know
the village was burned,"
said Pilar.
"After you left
some men came
looking for you.
They wanted me to tell them
where you went.
Of course, I didn't know.
So they beat me up.
After that happened,
we had to leave."

"Where did you go?"
Ramón asked her.

"A refugee camp
in Honduras,"
Pilar explained.
"10,000 people there.
It was bad.
Many people died there."

"How did you come
into this country?"
Ramon wondered.

"We left the camp,"
Pilar began.
"We hopped a train.
We hid in a boxcar.
We got across the U.S. border.
But we were caught right away.
We were taken
to a camp.
Then some good people
posted bonds for us.
We have had
sanctuary in Houston
ever since."

The Fullers
took the Samoya family
into their home.
Not long after that,
Pilar got a letter.
It was from a Salvadoran friend
living in Maryland.
She and her husband
had a restaurant there.
Would Pilar and Ramón
like to come north
and work in the restaurant?

The answer was "Yes!"
They thanked the Fullers
again and again
for all their help.

10 Cristina and Carlos

A growing number
of Salvadorans were living
in Washington, D.C.
and Maryland.
Ramón and Pilar Samoya
became part of this community.
Both of them
worked in the restaurant.
Pilar cooked.
Ramón helped
with everything.

They learned more English.
They had two more children.
All four children
went to school.
The family lived
like Americans.

Pilar's *pupusa**
was like a dish
she made in El Salvador.
"Best ever!"
said everyone who ate it.
So when the restaurant owners
wanted to leave the business,
Pilar and Ramón took over.
They gave the restaurant
a new name: Pupusa.

Then, in 1990,
a great thing happened.
Pilar and the two older children
got Temporary Protected Status,
or TPS.
This let them stay in the U.S.
because El Salvador
was not safe.
They got papers
to live and work
safely in Maryland.

* Pupusa *is a popular Salvadoran dish:
cornmeal griddlecake with cheese, spices,
beans, and pork.*

Later in that year,
Ramón became
a U.S. citizen.
The two younger children
were American citizens,
because they were born
in the United States.
Different papers,
all in one family.

The civil war
in El Salvador
ended in 1992.
But life in El Salvador
was still hard.
There were not enough jobs.
Many of the guerillas
became drug gangs.
They knew how to kill,
and the killing went on.

"We cannot go back,
even to visit,
until it is safe,"
said Ramón.
"We are building
a good life here.
We feel safe here."

Then, in 2001,
two big earthquakes
hit El Salvador.
Mud came down the mountains
and covered villages.
One out of four people
lost their home.
A thousand people died.
The country
was a mess.

"All Salvadorans
are our neighbors,"
said Ramón.
"We must help
our neighbors.
Like Barney and Sarah
helped us.
Like the nuns
in Arizona and Texas.
Like good people
all over the country."

"Our older children
are grown up now,"
said Pilar.
"We have enough room
for refugees.
Even if we had a full house,
we would make room!"

The Samoyas
took in a young mother
with a baby boy.
Pilar saw herself
in the young woman.
Her name was Cristina.
Her husband Carlos
had stayed in El Salvador
with an older son and daughter.
Cristina did not know
if they were safe.
Or even if they were alive.

Cristina found out
that her parents were safe.
But after the earthquakes
they had no work.

Cristina started working
at Pupusa.
She sent money
to her parents
to help them out.
Her parents
counted on that money,
month after month,
year after year.

No one in the house
would ever forget
"Carlos Day."
It was the day
they found out
that Carlos was safe.
And that he was trying
to come to Maryland.
Cristina cried for joy.
She would be so happy
to see her husband
and two older children.

But when Carlos came,
he came alone.

11 Valeria and Vittorio

Eight years later

Cristina and Carlos
went on living
with Ramón and Pilar.
They did not see
their two older children
for eight long years.

At last, word came
that the girl and boy
were on their way.
Cristina and Carlos
were so happy.

But trouble started
as soon as Valeria and Vittorio
got to Maryland.
They went to high school,
but they spoke no English.
They didn't fit in.
Worst of all,
after all these years,
they did not know their parents.

Cristina and Carlos
thought Valeria and Vittorio
were going to school
every morning.
But no.

When members
of the MS-13 street gang*
made friends with them,
Valeria and Vittorio
joined the gang.

They dressed
like the other gang members.
They got tattoos
on their arms, backs, and faces.
They all wore
the same kind of shoes.
And they all made
the same hand sign.
They spread their fingers
to look like devil's horns.

The gang made
Valeria and Vittorio do things they
didn't want to do.

* *MS = Mara Salvatrucha*

The brother and sister
were afraid.
But they could not leave the gang.
"You can never get out,"
they were told.

Valeria cooked and cleaned
for the gang.
Vittorio sold drugs.
He and the other boys
painted "MS-13"
on buildings.
One boy in the gang
became Valeria's boyfriend.

The boy's old girlfriend
did not like Valeria.
One day,
the old girlfriend
came after Valeria
with a knife.
Ten boys came with her.
They carried knives
and baseball bats.
Valeria cried out for help.
Vittorio heard her cry.

What happened next
was ugly and very sad.
A big knife fight broke out.
Valeria got away.
Vittorio did not.
He was cut badly.
He lay on the ground
with blood all around him.

After everyone ran away,
Valeria came back.
When the police came,
Valeria was alone,
crying over Vittorio's dead body.
The police drove her home
and told her parents
about Vittorio.

This was a hard time
for everyone.
"We will get you help,"
Ramón told Valeria.
"We love you.
Don't ever forget that."

Pilar worked with a group
helping kids get away
from MS-13.

"We will help you
to live clean,"
Pilar told Valeria.
"You will go back to school.
You will learn English.
You will get to know
your parents again."

More than anything,
Valeria wanted out of the gang.
But she was afraid.
So she joined the help group.
Starting a new life was hard.
Very, very hard.
But she knew what she wanted.
And what she didn't want.
She knew she needed help.

Cristina would never forget
the day Valeria kissed her.
It was the first time
in more than eight years.
"Thank you, Mama!"
Valeria said.
"I am home now."

12 The TPS Years

Thousands of people
from Central America,
and other countries
had been given TPS.
It was legal for them
to live and work in the U.S.

Back in El Salvador
there were storms,
floods, and earthquakes.
There were not enough homes.
Not enough jobs.
On top of that,
gangs were growing and killing.
There was no home
to go back to.
All they could do
was send money to loved ones.

Ramón, Pilar, and their friends
wrote letters to the president.
They begged to keep their TPS.

And so TPS went on.
Every 6, 12, or 18 months
people filled out papers
and paid fifty dollars
to stay in the U.S.

Through the TPS years,
Ramón and Pilar
worked long days
at their restaurant, Pupusa.
Their children grew up
and worked there too.
They had children
of their own.
The family
was living a good life.

Many older Salvadorans
were not American citizens.
But they had lived like Americans.
Young Salvadoran Americans
knew no other home.

All the while,
new people came to the U.S.
New neighbors.
New people to help.

In 2018,
everything turned upside-down.
The U.S. government
put an end to TPS.
Anyone with TPS
had 18 months
to return to their countries.
Two hundred thousand Salvadorans
had to return to El Salvador
or be deported.

"What are we going to do?"
Pilar asked Ramón.
"Some of us have TPS.
You are a U.S. citizen.
Two of our children
and all of our grandchildren
are U.S. citizens.
We would be torn apart!
What a mess we are in!"

Ramón put his arms
around his wife.
"We'll work this out,"
he said.
"I don't know how,
but we have to."

13 Going to Washington

One day,
out of the blue,
Sarah Fuller called.

"Remember me?"
she asked Ramón.

"Of course, I do!"
said Ramón.
"I'll never forget
all the help and love
you and Barney gave us
when we first came to the U.S."

"I have sad news,"
said Sarah.
"Barney passed away.
He was old.
He was so sick.
He's in a better place now."

"I'm so sorry!"
said Ramón.

"Barney had one last wish,"
Sarah went on.
"He knew
that your family
could be torn apart
if TPS ends.
He wanted you and Pilar
to go to Washington
and tell your family's story.
Some people in the government
were trying to save TPS.
They are listening to people
and getting information."

"Our English isn't so good,"
said Ramón.
"What would we say?"

"Just tell your story,"
Sarah told him.

Washington was not far away.
So Ramón and Pilar
took a bus
to the nation's capital.

They told their story
to a government committee.
They told about how
Ramón was caught
between the government
and the *guerillas*.
They told about how
he had gotten asylum
and later became a citizen.
How Pilar and the two children
came later and got TPS.
How Cristina and Carlos
did not see their children
for eight years.
How the Salvadorans
worked hard and paid taxes.
How they sent money
to help their families
in El Salvador.
How some of their children
were born as U.S. citizens.
How their family
would be torn apart
if TPS ended.

"Life in El Salvador
was very bad
when I left 38 years ago,"
Ramón said.
"But it is worse now.
There is very little work.
Gangs make young people join
or they kill them.
With all our hearts
we want to stay safe.
We want to do that
only here."

The committee listened.
They heard the stories
of real people.

Outside,
people carried signs:

SAVE TPS
I'M HERE
FOR OUR DREAM

Children wore T-shirts:

DON'T DEPORT MY DAD
DON'T DEPORT MY MOM

A ray of hope
came a few months later.
A court in California
stopped the government
from stopping TPS.
This was not
the end of the story.
But it was one step closer
in keeping families together.

14　José and Gabriela

The Samoyas
were together,
for now.
But other families
were being torn apart
in a different way.

Thousands of people
were leaving Central America.
They hoped to get
asylum in the U.S.

One of them
was Ramón's brother's son.
His name was José.
He had a four-year-old daughter.
Her name was Gabriela.
José carried Gabriela
as he walked
toward the U.S. border.
Some days they climbed
into the back of a truck.
At last, months later,
they reached the U.S. border.

José carried Gabriela
as they waited in line
to apply for asylum.
He held her tight.
She rested her head
on his face.

"Come with me,"
a border patrol said to Gabriela.
"We'll give you a bath
while your papa waits."

She held her father
even tighter.
She began to cry.

"We must do
what they tell us,"
José told her.
"See you soon!
Don't be afraid!
I love you!"

With a heavy heart
José kissed his little girl.
Then he handed her over
to the border patrol.

Gabriela cried even more.
She reached out her arms
and cried, "Papa! Papa!"

José would not see Gabriela
for a long, long time.
He did not get
an asylum hearing.
After several weeks in jail
he was deported,
sent back to El Salvador.
Gabriela was sent
to a center for children.
A place where she knew no one.
A place where no one
could touch her.
Where she slept
in a little cage.
Where she cried "Papa! Papa!"
day and night.

Ramón and Pilar
did not hear from José.
They had no idea
what had happened.

They made phone calls.
They wrote letters.
No answers.

At last José called
from El Salvador.
He told them
what had happened
at the border.
He still did not know
where his daughter was.
She had no ID.
How could he find her?

"We will find her,"
Ramón told José.
"We will bring her
to Maryland.
We will take care of her.
We will love her
until you are together again."

"*Gracias, mi tío*!"
José cried into the phone.

*Spanish: "Thank you, my uncle!"

Back in El Salvador,
José did farm work
for five dollars a day.
He waited to hear
about his daughter.

In Maryland,
Ramón tried to find Gabriela.
There were children's centers
all over the country.
Where could this little girl be?
Ramón did not even know
what she looked like.
Only her name.

So when José
sent Gabriela's picture,
Ramón sent it to Sarah Fuller.
She was in Texas.
So was a center
full of little girls.

Once again,
Sarah was a good neighbor.
She found little Gabriela!
And then she brought her
all the way to Maryland.

15 The Festival

Sarah and Gabriela
came to Maryland
at just the right time.
Once a year,
the Salvadoran-Americans
held a big festival.
Thousands of people came.
The Samoyas were there
with Cristina, Carlos, Valeria,
Gabriela, and Sarah.

What a day!
Salvadoran music
filled the air.
Salvadoran food
filled their noses and stomachs.
Thousands of people
filled their hearts.
Everyone speaking Spanish!

Laughing!
Singing!
Dancing!
Fireworks!

For one day
they threw away their cares.
They did not worry
about what would happen
to their families
if they lost TPS.
They did not worry
about deportation.
They did not worry
about crossing the border.
They did not worry
about the gangs.

They did not forget
all these troubles.
They would come back
tomorrow and the days after that.
But today,
everyone was having fun.
They sang along
with the music.

They danced *cumbia** and hip hop.
They were neighbors,
today and always.

Then Ramón stood
before the crowd.
"I have good news!"
he began.
"Many of you
are too young to remember
Óscar Romero.
He was Archbishop of San Salvador.
He stood up for the poor,
for us, for our neighbors.
He was killed
for speaking out
against the civil war
in El Salvador.
He died for us
many years ago.
He was a good neighbor.

* Cumbia *is a folk dance that began in Colombia.*
South and Central American countries each
have their own version.

Now, he has become a saint.
The first saint
from El Salvador!"

The crowd cheered.

"As I speak,"
Ramón went on,
"Central Americans
are leaving their countries
to save their lives.
I know their fear.
I know their pain.
We pray for our neighbors!
May God keep them safe!"

Ramón stepped down.
He hugged Pilar
and everyone else in sight.
And running around inside his head
he saw the white *cadejo*.
He smiled,
with hope in his heart.

Glossary

Definitions and examples of certain words and
terms used in the story

Chapter 1 ✢ Ramón and Pilar (page 1)

Archbishop – An important position in
the Catholic church.
*Omar Romero. Archbishop of San
Salvador ...*

mass – The main public religious
celebration of the Catholic church.
*... [the] Archbishop had more than
mass to say today.*

thou shalt – An older, more formal
pronoun for "you," and an older
form of the verb "shall."
Thou shalt not kill.

all of a sudden – Suddenly.
All of a sudden a man burst in.

burst in – to enter a place suddenly.
All of a sudden a man burst in.

spread – To go out from a place in all
　　directions.
　　The news ... spread throughout
　　El Salvador.

campesinos – Small peasant farmers.
　　The Samoyas were young campesinos.

mud – Wet dirt or earth.When it dries it can
　　be used to make walls for a simple
　　house.
　　Their house was made of sticks and
　　mud.

ground (grind) – To break or mash (corn)
　　into a powder for making bread.
　　She ground corn with a rock.

civil war – A war within a single country
　　where citizens of the country are
　　fighting each other.
　　Ramon and Pilar knew about the
　　civil war.

squad – A small group of soldiers or police.
　　A death squad killed the archbishop.

guerillas – A group of fighters who fight against the government. In Spanish *guerra* is "war."
Then there are the guerillas.

what's going on – What is happening, the situation, at the moment.
Maybe now the world will hear what's going on in El Salvador.

Chapter 2 ✢ Felipe (page 6)

word got around – The news became known everywhere.
But word got around, from person to person, from village to village.

speaking out – Complaining; demanding.
Some were killed for speaking out.

force – Power, strength.
The force of evil.

in no time at all – very fast; quick.
In no time at all the little house was a ball of fire.

Chapter 3 ✛ The Land (page 10)

carried (carry) on – To continue.
Village life carried on.

found out – To learn or discover something.
What if the wrong people found out?

never dreamed of – To not think or believe
something could be possible ...
*Ramon did something he had never
dreamed of.*

Chapter 4 ✛ An Old Neighbor (page 14)

get out of – To leave; go away.
You will get out of here.

cool off – To quiet down and be less
dangerous.
*I will come back as soon as things
cool off.*

Chapter 5 ✛ Leaving the Country (page 18)

marked for death – Threatened with death.
But he would be safer than a man marked for death.

the sign of the cross – A Catholic gesture made by the hand touching the forehead, the chest, and the shoulders.
He made the sign of the cross.

over his head – Unable to touch the ground.
It was not deep, but it was over his head.

Chapter 6 ✛ Back Again (page 22)

coyote – A person who will take people across the border for a fee.
Ramon decided to pay a coyote …

pulled away – Left (to leave).
The van pulled away.

on their own – To have no help.
They were on their own now.

Chapter 7 ✢ Two Nuns (page 25)

nuns – Women who work for the Catholic
church to serve people.
*Two young nuns got out and handed
out water.*

a safe house – A place where people can hide.
This is a safe house ...

Chapter 8 ✢ Barney and Sarah (page 29)

bad shape – Poor condition or health.
Ramón was in bad shape.

sanctuary – A place where one is safe from
harm.
*... a family in Texas would give him
sanctuary.*

got (get) by – Able to have simple or basic
communication.
*But they and Ramón got by
with just a few words.*

fit in – To be comfortable with a situation
or place.
Still, he didn't fit in.

Chapter 9 ✤ Pilar's Story (page 35)

beat (me) up – To hurt someone by
hitting them hard and often.
So they beat me up.

boxcar – A car that is part of a freight
train. It has large sliding doors.
We hid in a boxcar.

right away – Immediately.
But we were caught right away.

posted bonds – Paying to get someone
out of a jail.
Some good people posted bonds for us.

hopped – To get on a train without a ticket.
We hopped a train.

Chapter 10 ✦ Cristina and Carlos (page 39)

took (take) over – To become the owner
   or leader of something.
   Pilar and Ramón took over.

took (take) in – To give living space
   to someone.
   The Samoyas took in a young mother.

saw (see) herself – To see a person's
   situation as similar to one's own.
   Pilar saw herself in the young woman.

help (someone) out – To give help.
   She sent money ... to help them out.

counted (count) on – To depend on;
   to plan for.
   Her parents counted on that money.

Chapter 11 ✤ Valeria and Vittorio (page 45)

went on – Continued.
> *Cristina and Carlos went on living
> with Ramón and Pilar.*

on their way – Somewhere along the route.
> *... word came that the girl and boy
> were on their way.*

get out – To leave a place or organization.
> *You can never get out.*

broke out – Began suddenly.
> *A big knife fight broke out.*

got away – Escaped.
> *Valeria got away.*

Chapter 12 ✛ The TPR Years (page 50)

on top of that – Also; besides; in addition.
*On top of that, gangs were growing
and killing.*

all the while – Day after day; continuously.
*All the while, new people came
to the U.S.*

turned upside-down – A big change,
usually not good.
Everything turned upside-down.

torn apart – Separated in a bad way.
We would be torn apart!

Chapter 13 ✛ Going to Washington (page 53)

out of the blue – Unexpected.
  *One day, out of the blue, Sarah
  Fuller called.*

passed away – Died.
  Barney passed away.

told about how – Described; gave
  information.
  *They told about how Ramón was
  caught.*

a ray (of hope) – Like light from the sun.
  *A ray of hope came a few
  months later.*

Chapter 14 ✤ Jose and Gabriela (page 58)

hand over – To give someone to
    someone else.
    *Then he handed her over to the
    border patrol.*

hearing – A formal time to explain and
    ask for something.
    He did not get an asylum hearing.

cage – A small box, usually metal,
    usually for animals.
    ... she slept in a little cage.

Chapter 15 ✤ The Festival (page 63)

threw (throw) away – To toss out;
    to forget about.
    *For one day they threw away
    their cares.*